Stolen Stanley Cup

PETER PUCK

and the

Stolen Stanley Cup

BRIAN McFARLANE
illustrated by **GERI STOREY**

FENN

TUNDRA

Published in Canada by Tundra of Tundra Books,
a division of Random House of Canada Limited
One Toronto Street, Suite 300, Toronto, Ontario M5C 2V6

Published in the United States by Tundra Books of Northern New York,
P.O. Box 1030, Plattsburgh, New York 12901

Library of Congress Control Number: 2013953678

Library and Archives Canada Cataloguing in Publication

McFarlane, Brian, 1931-, author
Peter Puck and the stolen Stanley Cup / by Brian McFarlane ;
illustrated by Geri Storey.

(The adventures of hockey's greatest mascot)
Previously published: Peter Puck and the stolen Stanley Cup / by Brian McFarlane ;
drawings by Bill Reid. — Willowdale, Ont. : Library Shoppe, c1980.
Issued in print and electronic formats.
ISBN 978-1-77049-581-4 (bound).—ISBN 978-1-77049-582-1 (epub)

I. Storey, Geri, illustrator II. Title.

PS8575.F37P47 2015   jC813'.54   C2013-906929-1
                                                C2013-906930-5

Edited by Debbie Rogosin
The text was set in Fairfield.
www.tundrabooks.com

Printed and bound in China

1 2 3 4 5 6   20 19 18 17 16 15

Contents

CHAPTER 1

A Playoff Game

Whack! Zap! Crunch!

Peter Puck was taking a pounding, but he didn't mind. He was right where he belonged, in the middle of one of the biggest hockey games of the year.

It was the sixth game of the Stanley Cup

playoffs. The Metro City Scouts were playing the Winston Warriors in the Warriors' arena. With a victory tonight, the rough, tough home team could win the Stanley Cup.

Peter was the most famous puck in hockey, and he had been in plenty of playoff games. But he couldn't recall a more exciting series.

Sticks poked at Peter and smacked him. He bounced off skates, pads, and the boards. He was sent flying into the glass behind the nets with such speed that some fans screamed and ducked. A puck couldn't ask for more fun.

Butch Burns, the Warriors' goalie, egged his team on. "Give it to them, boys," he shouted. "And when the Scouts shoot Peter Puck my way, I'll take care of the rubber rascal. He'll look like a skid mark on the highway when I get through with him."

Peter noticed that the goalie's mask had a snarling tiger painted on the top. And Burns had attached a fake tiger tail to the back of his mask. It hung down like a ponytail. He's always looking for attention, Peter thought. What a show-off.

The game was scoreless until the middle of the third period. Then a Warriors' winger got a breakaway. He came in alone, shot – and scored!

"Whoopee! It's 1–0 for the good guys," goalie Burns called out to the Scouts' bench. "I'm great, great, great, and I'm headed for a shutout!"

The Scouts' captain, Steve Swift, heard the goalie's taunts. When the puck was dropped he snared Peter with his stick and dashed up the ice. The defense screened their goalie, but Swift let go a shot that rocketed past Burns and into the net.

The score was tied, 1–1!

Burns was furious. He banged his stick on the crossbar and jumped up and down. But when he accidentally stepped on Peter in the crease …

Whump! Burns lost his balance and fell on the seat of his pants.

Everybody laughed.

Serves you right, you poor sport, Peter thought.

Minutes later, Steve Swift struck again. He skated in, scooted between the defensemen, and scored a pretty goal that gave the Scouts the lead.

The Warriors tried hard to score. But the Scouts hung on to win the game, 2–1. The series was tied. There would be a seventh and deciding game for the Stanley Cup. And it would be played on the Scouts' home ice.

CHAPTER 2

The Cup Disappears

The next day, Peter found himself high in the air aboard a plane. He was traveling to Metro City with his pal, referee George Phair.

Peter loved to fly.

Passengers who saw Peter recognized the

famous puck. Often they stopped to say hello and get an autograph.

"Hi, Peter. I'm a big fan of yours."

"Have a good game tomorrow, Mr. Puck."

And if Peter curled up and took a nap, George Phair made sure nobody sat on him by mistake.

"Why me, George?" Peter asked the referee. "You could have picked any number of pucks for the big game."

"It's because you're number one with the referees, Pete. You're a real pro. We need a puck like you for the biggest game of the season."

Peter beamed. "Thanks, George. I think you're great, too. Your nickname says it all — George 'Always' Phair. Say, who do you think will win the big game tomorrow night?"

"Referees never make predictions or take

sides, Pete. You know that. Anything can happen in hockey."

It was almost midnight when the plane landed in Metro City. George Phair took Peter right to the arena. The building was locked, but George went to a special door and rang a buzzer. The security guard, Jess Jackson, let them in.

"Hi, Pete. Hi, George," said Jess. "I was expecting you." He led them down a corridor and through the lobby. They passed a large glass showcase that held a gleaming trophy.

"Is that what I think it is?" Peter asked. He went over for a closer look. "It is! It's the Stanley Cup!"

His companions laughed.

"Indeed it is," said Jess Jackson. "It's all polished and ready to be presented to the winning team tomorrow night. And during the day, fans will be able to have their photos taken with the Cup."

"It's a beauty, isn't it?" said the referee. "It's the oldest team trophy in the world, and it's priceless."

"Will it be safe here tonight?" Peter asked.

Jess Jackson laughed. "It sure will. The showcase is locked, and I have the key in my

pocket. All the arena doors are locked, too. And just in case, I'll be up all night, keeping an eye on it."

They reached the room where the freezer was kept. Hockey pucks are kept in a freezer before games. It takes some of the bounce out of their hard rubber bodies.

Peter hopped into the freezer and wished his friends good night. As they left the room, George said to Jess, "I'm sure glad refs don't have to sleep in a freezer."

"Peter never complains," said Jess. "The freezer is one place a puck can find a little peace and quiet."

George waved good-bye and left the arena. Jess returned to the lobby to guard the Stanley Cup.

Hours passed. Suddenly, Peter woke up. Something was wrong. He was sweating.

Peter jumped up in alarm and threw open the freezer door. The room was full of smoke and flames. A fire alarm was blaring. "Fire!" he shouted. "Help!"

Seconds later, Jess Jackson rushed in. He pulled Peter to safety. Then he took a fire extinguisher to the blaze.

When the fire was out, Peter jumped onto the guard's shoulder.

"Thanks, my friend. If you hadn't rescued me, I'd be a puddle of rubber by now. What happened, Jess?"

Jess shrugged. "Pete, there must be somebody else in the arena. And that person is up to no good. The fire was started on purpose."

Suddenly they heard a loud crash.

"What was that?" Peter asked.

"That was the showcase in the lobby,"

Jess shouted. "Somebody's trying to steal the Stanley Cup. Come on, Pete. We have to stop the thief."

Peter and Jess raced to the lobby. The floor was covered with broken glass, but nobody was there.

"Oh, no!" cried Peter. "The Cup is gone!"

Jess said, "Listen. Do you hear that thumping? Someone is running away."

"The robber can't get far lugging that big thing," shouted Peter. "Let's catch the rascal."

They followed the sound of the footsteps. Jess was in the lead, but soon he was breathing hard. Peter tugged on his pant leg. "Take it easy, Jess. I'm in better shape than you. I'll keep up the chase while you phone the police."

"Okay, Pete," said the guard. "But be careful. I caught a glimpse of him. He's a big fellow."

Peter kept on running.

In the dark, he almost tripped over something. It was a goalie skate. "Aha," Peter muttered to himself. "I bet the thief used it to break the glass in the showcase." He pushed the skate aside and raced on.

Ahead, he saw a shaft of light. The thief was pushing the Stanley Cup through an exit door.

Peter put on a burst of speed and headed out the door after him.

The burglar saw Peter and put down the trophy. He grabbed a garbage can and swung it at Peter, bowling him over. Then he took the can and slammed it down, trapping Peter inside.

Peter banged on the inside of the can with his tiny knuckles. "Help, Jess! I need help."

There was no answer.

Peter squeezed his fingers under the lip of the can. Using all his strength, he lifted it over his head, and it rolled away. Peter hurried after the thief, but it was too late.

Jess appeared a few minutes later. "What happened, Pete?" he asked. "Did the thief get away?"

"Yes," Peter told him sadly. "I didn't see his face, but I saw his hair. He had a ponytail. He took off in a car."

"I'm in trouble now," moaned Jess. "Wait until the media people hear about this."

CHAPTER 3

Who Stole the Cup?

It wasn't long before everybody knew about the theft of the Stanley Cup. The police arrived and began to question Jess and Peter. Reporters and TV camera crews were right behind.

A woman from NHL security arrived, still wearing her pajamas and slippers. She was

upset with Jess and Peter. "What happened? How could you lose hockey's most famous trophy? You'd better hope it shows up in time for the big game."

"Please don't blame Jess," Peter urged. "He saved me from being roasted. And he tried to save the Cup. He's a real hero."

"Peter's an even bigger hero," Jess insisted. "He's the bravest little guy around. He chased that big fellow right out of the arena."

When the police and the reporters talked to Peter, he told them everything he could remember. He even mentioned the goalie skate. Maybe the police would find fingerprints on it.

"You were very brave to try and stop the thief," one of the reporters said.

For the rest of the morning, Peter wasn't thinking about being brave. He was too busy doing some detective work of his own. Maybe he could help the police find the Stanley Cup.

First he asked both Zamboni Ice Resurfacing Machines if they'd seen or heard anything during the night.

"Sorry, Pete. We had a long day of ice making. We slept like babies."

He put the same question to the big time clock over center ice.

"I'd like to give you a hand," was the grumpy reply. "But I haven't got time for this."

Oh, brother, thought Peter. A clock with no time. And only one hand.

Peter went back to Jess and asked if he'd seen anything suspicious during the night.

"Anything at all, Jess?"

The security guard put a hand to his chin. Suddenly, he snapped his fingers. "I just remembered. Something did happen. A car drove up last night and a young fellow got out and knocked on the door. Said he was a Warriors' player and wanted to make sure all his equipment had arrived. Earlier, the airline had lost some of his gear."

"Did you ask him his name, Jess?"

"No, but he was wearing a Warriors' jacket and he looked familiar, so I let him in. We went to the visitors' dressing room, and all his equipment was there. He seemed relieved, but he was nervous. Pre-game jitters, I figured. So I offered to make him a coffee. When I came back with the coffee he was gone."

"Was his car gone, too?"

"Yes, I checked."

"Do you think it's possible that he drove around the corner to hide the car and then sneaked back in?"

"Maybe. It took me a while to heat the water for the coffee."

"Can you remember anything else about him, Jess?"

"One thing. There were some big letters on the back of his jacket – WGG. He just laughed when I asked what the letters stood for."

Hmmm, thought Peter. WGG.

CHAPTER 4

The Final Game

*T*he huge arena was buzzing with excitement when referee George Phair skated to center ice with Peter Puck in his hand. Peter got a big round of applause from the fans. They had heard about his overnight adventure and his brave effort to save the Stanley Cup.

"Here we go, Pete," George said. "It's game time."

Skates flashed across the ice as the players chased after Peter. The crowd cheered when the Scouts' goalie, Charlie Stopper, turned aside several shots. They booed when the Warriors' goalie, Butch Burns, argued with the referee.

"Ref, he knocked me down."

George Phair didn't agree. "No, you jumped in front of him, Burns. Then you took a dive. You rolled around the ice like your pants were on fire, pretending to be hurt. No penalty."

When the referee's back was turned, Burns stuck out his tongue.

The game continued, with non-stop action and superb playing from both sides.

With two minutes left in the second

period, there was still no score. Then the Warriors got a lucky break. A shot bounced off Charlie Stopper's pads. The Scouts' captain tried to bat the rebound away. But the puck hit a skate, changed direction, and slipped through the goalie's legs.

Steve Swift had scored on his own goalie!

The Scouts' fans groaned.

The third period opened with the Warriors in the lead, 1–0. Peter could hear Butch Burns gloating. "I'm going to win the Cup," he sang out. He circled his net doing a victory dance.

His antics had the Scouts fuming. But try as they might, they could not score. With a minute left to play, the Scouts were running out of energy. A time-out was called, and Steve Swift turned to his coach.

"I'm so tired I can barely skate," he gasped.

"A real pro never gives up, Steve," the coach urged. "You must have a little bit left in your gas tank."

Swift gave a little grin. "Thanks, Coach," he said.

When the puck was dropped, Swift snared it. He charged at the defense. Crash Cranston and Slugger Simpson waited, ready to pounce on him.

Swift hesitated at the blue line. It looked like he wanted to avoid the two tough defenders.

"We've got him!" snarled Cranston.

"He's scared stiff!" whooped Simpson.

But Swift wasn't afraid. He was looking for an opening between the pair. He found one and slipped through. What a move! Then in one motion he fired a slap shot that buzzed by Butch Burns' ear.

Goal!

Tie game!

Fans went wild. Programs sailed out onto the ice. Music blared.

Men with scrapers came out to clean up the litter. They popped Peter on top of Burns' goal net, to get him out of their way.

That's when Peter saw the tiger tail Burns had fastened to the back of his helmet. And the letters WGG just above it.

"That's what I saw last night," Peter muttered. "I thought the thief had a ponytail, but it was a tiger tail. And the letters WGG probably stand for World's Greatest Goalie. Only Burns would claim to be the greatest."

George Phair skated by and plucked Peter from the net.

"Time for one more face-off, Pete."

Once again, Swift won the draw. With a great burst of speed, he deked around Cranston and Simpson.

He wound up for another slap shot. Burns charged at Swift and sprawled to stop the shot. But there was no shot. Swift calmly skated around him and slipped the puck into the open net.

With that last-second goal, the Scouts won the game – and the Stanley Cup!

While the Scouts celebrated their victory and the crowd went wild, Peter Puck found himself in danger. Butch Burns was angry, and he was going to take it out on Peter. He raised his big goalie stick.

Peter scurried away. He zipped around the net with Burns chasing after him. Around and around they went. Just when Burns was about to pounce on him, Peter stopped right in front of the goalie's skates.

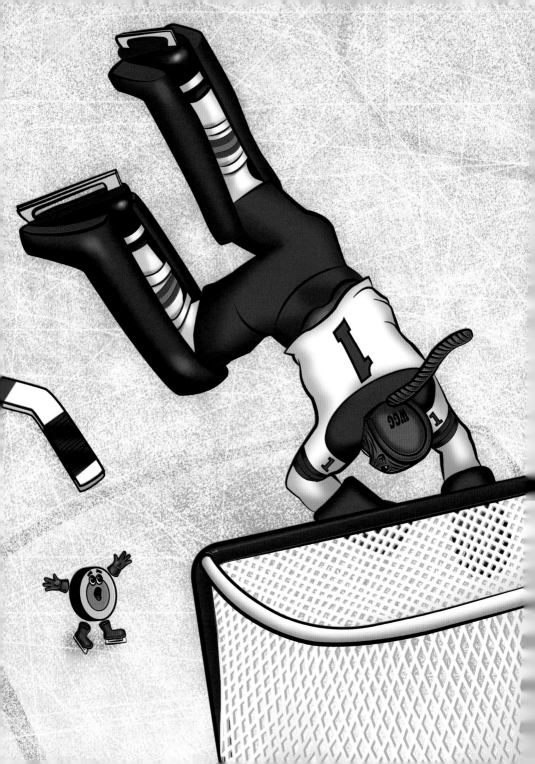

Crash!

Burns did an amazing somersault right over Peter and flew into the empty net. The net came loose and fell over, and Burns was trapped.

Peter flipped himself onto the net while players and officials gathered around.

"Got you now, Mr. Burns," cried Peter. "I know you stole the Stanley Cup. Your tiger tail gave you away. And the letters WGG."

"That's no proof," Burns scoffed. "And you don't know what WGG stands for."

"I bet I do. World's Greatest Goalie. But World's Greatest Goofball is more like it. And I'll bet your fingerprints are all over that goalie skate you used to break into the showcase," Peter continued. "You're not getting out of this net until you confess."

Burns sighed. "You win, Pete. I admit it. I

stole the Cup. I didn't think our team could win it fair and square. And some of my pals dared me to do it. So I sneaked into the arena last night and stole the Cup. Thought I'd keep it for a few days. Maybe get my photo taken with it."

"What about the fire you started, Butch? You might have burned down the arena. And turned me into a puckburger."

"It was a big mistake, Pete. I wanted to distract the guard. I planned to sneak off with the Cup while he put out the fire. I didn't know you were asleep in the freezer. And I didn't mean to hurt anyone. Honest. I'm sorry."

"Well, you should be sorry, Butch. You need to play fair, on and off the ice."

Steve Swift leaned in. "Where's the Cup now, buddy?" he asked. "We won it and we want to see it."

"It's in the parking lot, in the trunk of a car I rented," Butch confessed. "Let me up and I'll get it."

"I'll go with you," said George Phair. "With some police officers. Just in case."

Minutes later, a great cheer went up when George Phair handed the Cup over to the league official. The official presented the Cup to Steve Swift, who held it high as he skated around the arena. The crowd cheered even louder.

Peter beamed. He had helped to get the Cup back, and just in time.

Meanwhile, a very remorseful Butch Burns was being led away by two police officers.

Then Steve motioned to Peter. "Hop in, Pete, and I'll take you for a ride. We wouldn't have the Cup if it weren't for you."

Peter Puck, so proud that he thought he might burst out of his rubber skin, took a great leap and landed in the bowl of the

Stanley Cup. Applause filled the arena when Steve paraded him around the ice.

Hockey is the greatest game of all, thought Peter. And the greatest feeling of all is taking a Stanley Cup victory lap. "This is it – the ride of a lifetime!" he said to Steve, as he waved to the crowd.

Join Peter on another adventure!

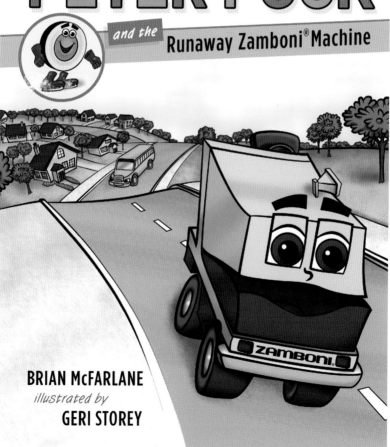

The Adventures of Hockey's Greatest Mascot

PETER PUCK

and the Runaway Zamboni® Machine

BRIAN McFARLANE

illustrated by

GERI STOREY